KU-449-164

Dray's farm

Apple Tree
Station

Apple Tree
Village

Church

School

Manor

Farmyard Tales

Pig Gets Stuck

Heather Amery

Illustrated by Stephen Cartwright

Adapted by Anna Milbourne

Reading consultant: Alison Kelly

Find the duck on every double page.

This story is about
Apple Tree Farm,

Mrs. Boot
the farmer,

Poppy,

Sam,

 hens,

cows,

 a horse,

Curly

and some other pigs.

It was a busy morning at Apple Tree Farm.

Let's feed the animals!

Curly, the smallest
pig, was waiting for
breakfast.

He was very hungry.

The bigger pigs gobbled everything up.

Poor little Curly didn't get any food.

So he squeezed under
the fence to find some.

He looked at the
cows' breakfast.

He looked at the
sheep's breakfast.

He looked at the
horse's breakfast.

Then he saw the
hens' breakfast.

It looked tasty.

Curly squeezed through
a gap in the fence.

He gobbled up the
hens' breakfast, every
last scrap.

Then Mrs. Boot found
him.

Curly tried to run away

but he'd eaten too
much. He couldn't fit
through the gap.

He was stuck! Poppy
and Sam came to help.

Curly looks
funny!

They tried to push him
free, but he squealed.

At last, he popped out
with a grunt.

Mrs. Boot gave him
a cuddle.

Poor little pig.

They took Curly home
to his pig pen.

"You'll have lots of
breakfast tomorrow,"
Mrs. Boot said.

And he did!

Puzzles

Puzzle 1

Put these pictures in the right order to tell the story.

A.

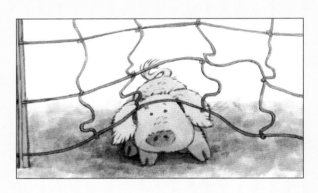

B.

C.

D.

E.

23

Puzzle 2

Can you find these things in the picture?

hens   pig   fence

dog   dish

Puzzle 3

Can you spot six differences
between these two pictures?

Puzzle 4

Choose the right speech bubble for each picture.

A.

27

Answers to puzzles
Puzzle 1

1C.

2A.

3E.

4D.

5B.

Puzzle 2

dog

pig

fence

hens

dish

29

Puzzle 3

Puzzle 4

A.

B.

C.

Designed by Laura Nelson
Series editor: Lesley Sims
Series designer: Russell Punter
Digital manipulation by Nick Wakeford

This edition first published in 2015 by Usborne Publishing Ltd.,
Usborne House, 83-85 Saffron Hill, London EC1N 8RT, England.
www.usborne.com Copyright © 2015, 1989 Usborne Publishing Ltd.

USBORNE FIRST READING
Level Two

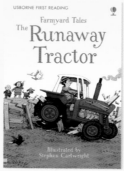

Farmyard Tales
The **Runaway Tractor**

Illustrated by
Stephen Cartwright

How Elephants lost their Wings

Retold by
Lesley Sims
Illustrated by Katie Lovell

Little Miss Muffet

Retold by Russell Punter
Illustrated by Lorena Alvarez

THE STONECUTTER

RETOLD BY LYNNE BENTON
ILLUSTRATED BY LEE COSGROVE

Old Mother Hubbard

Retold by Russell Punter
Illustrated by Fred Blunt

One, Two, Buckle My Shoe

Retold by Russell Punter
Illustrated by David Semple

There Was A Crooked Man

Retold by
Russell Punter
Illustrated by David Semple

The **Baobab Tree**

Retold by Laura Stowell
Illustrated by Laure Fournier

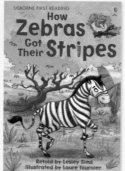

How **Zebras Got Their Stripes**

Retold by Lesley Sims
Illustrated by Laure Fournier